Ice Palace

by **Deborah Blumenthal**

illustrated by **Ted Rand**

Clarion Books ❄ New York

Special thanks go to Saranac Lake resident and photographer Mark Kurtz
for his research assistance in the book's illustrations. —T.R.

Clarion Books
a Houghton Mifflin Company imprint
215 Park Avenue South, New York, NY 10003
The text was set in 16.5-point ITC Century Book Condensed.
The illustrations were executed in watercolor and acrylic paint.
www.houghtonmifflinbooks.com

Manufactured in China.

Library of Congress Cataloging-in-Publication Data
Blumenthal, Deborah
Ice palace / by Deborah Blumenthal ; [illustrated by] Ted Rand.
p.   cm.
Summary: A girl and her father help plan the annual winter carnival in
Saranac Lake, New York, as the girl's uncle and other prisoners
work together to build its centerpiece, the ice palace.
ISBN 0-618-15960-6
[1. Winter festivals—Fiction. 2. Festivals—Fiction. 3. Saranac Lake
(N.Y.)—Fiction.] I. Rand, Ted, ill. II. Title.
PZ7.B6267 Ic 2003
[Fic]—dc21
2002155648

SCP   10 9 8 7 6 5 4 3 2 1

To Annie, Sophie, and Ralph
—D.B.

In Saranac Lake village,
when water hardens into ice
and the wind blows as fierce
as the bite of an Adirondack black bear,
my father and I sit down
with other townspeople in a café.
We drink hot chocolate and coffee,
then click open ballpoint pens
and on paper napkins as thin as snowflakes
sketch out plans for the winter carnival.

There will be an ice palace, with high-pitched walls
and saw-toothed towers.
There will be a court for snowshoe volleyball,
and slopes for torchlight skiing,
and the four-mile Ice Palace Fun Run—
a slippery slide
like an icy chute
from the board of Chutes and Ladders.

Running the carnival is hard work,
but the hardest work comes before it begins.
On the way home from school
my father and I go to the ice field on Pontiac Bay on Lake Flower.
We see ice being scissored up
with a circular saw
that whines and buzzes its way down through twelve frozen inches.
Then workers cut into the grid with big handsaws,
carving out two-by-four-foot chunks
like a giant's toy blocks.
Each one can weigh as much as 800 pounds.

Cutting through a frozen lake isn't everyone's favorite kind of work.
And when it's down deep below zero—
the kind of weather that kills even germs—
it's hard to imagine, my father says,
that they can build up a good sweat, but they do.

I watch as the ice blocks are floated off the lake
along a watery channel.
An excavator, a big machine
that looks like a steam shovel,
grabs each block in its metal jaws
and sets it in the bucket of a small tractor
that carries them to the site,
across the way from the fast-food place.

To keep the blocks from sliding off each other,
the men fix them in place with nature's mortar—
slush that comes in five-gallon buckets
and freezes on contact with the ice.
The blocks are stacked one on top of the other,
and soon a wall takes shape.
Palace walls can be as high as sixty feet.

Dressed in bulky coats and pulled-down hats,
and wearing bright orange slush gloves
to keep out the punishing cold and damp,
the workers learn to do something they've never done before.
And for some men, my father says,
putting one block
neatly over another
and then another
until the blocks turn into the wall of a great palace
changes the way they see life,
at least for a while,
and makes them feel good about who they are.

It will take about two weeks to build the palace.
And every day
after school,
at least for a little while,
we stand outside and watch the crew work.
It's a big group,
and they all work together.
One of them is my Uncle Mike.

They don't talk much.
It seems they don't have to.
Each looks as if he knows what his job is—
sort of the way a softball team,
or even a family, works together,
everyone doing his own part
and knowing that he can depend on the others for help.

Sometimes, the harder the job,
the better it can make you feel in the end.
Like when I helped my father, who's a carpenter,
build a new porch on our neighbor's house,
or the time our pickup got stuck in a snowbank,
and I helped Dad and Uncle Mike
push it out.

Working with ice has a long tradition
in Saranac Lake.
In school we learned that the village
was the center of an ice industry
before there were electric refrigerators.
Back then
huge blocks of ice
were shipped far away
to places that weren't as cold,
to keep food safe in iceboxes
all around the country,
and outside it.

Maybe even back then
the men who carved up the ice
and hauled it out of the lake,
stomping their feet,
breathing frosty breath,
and rubbing their hands together,
had some of the same feelings
that these men do today.

Except some of these men are different
from the men who worked here
when ice was a business.
That's because some of the men building the ice palace now
live in a camp.
But not the kind made for sports and fun.

Camp Gabriels is a prison,
a place that keeps men away from other people for a while
because they've broken the law.
My uncle has been there for almost three months now,
with three more months to go.
Every day that I show up, he looks over at me with a small smile.
I think he likes to know that there's family nearby.

When our toes start to feel numb,
my father calls out goodbye to Uncle Mike
and takes my hand.
We walk to the fast-food place
and sit down and have a juicy hamburger
and crisp fries.
We count the days until the carnival begins.
I've been to ten carnivals,
starting the year I was born.

When opening day finally comes,
everyone is at the town hall for the coronation
of the king and queen of the carnival.
This year a volunteer firefighter is crowned king
because he's become like a dad
to kids who don't have a dad of their own.
A pediatrician is crowned queen
for working, after work,
with kids who have trouble learning.

For all ten days of the carnival
my father and I go to the events.
We watch ski races,
skating races,
hockey games,
volleyball that's played
in knee-deep snow,
and softball played in snowshoes
that can twist up your feet
and make you tumble over.
My friends and I practice those sports after school
because we know that in a few years
we'll be the ones the crowd is watching
and cheering for.

At the end of the carnival there's a big parade.
Everyone wears a funny costume.
Some march, some ride on floats.
Last year I wore a crazy-colored jester's hat and coat.
This year I'm dressed as a snowman.

23

It all ends with a giant fireworks display
over the ice palace.
We gaze up, hypnotized by the colored lights
that crackle, pop, and then splinter
into the dark sky.
In the confetti light, the ice glistens a thousand colors.

When we get home,
my father tucks me into bed.
He tells me about one of the men who built the ice palace,
how he asked if he could come back again
next year
to do the work—
even though by then he'll be out of prison
and free to do,
or not do,
whatever he wants.

I know that it was more than the hot coffee
and the rich chocolate doughnuts
that the men enjoyed on their rest breaks.
And it was more than the big dinner
for everyone who helped put the carnival together,
even though they enjoyed the food and the company.
And it was more than the certificates they took back to prison,
showing that the town appreciated all their hard work.

Maybe it was something
about doing a tough job,
honest work,
and, in the end,
having the job turn out just right
that made them hold themselves a little straighter.

I thought about Uncle Mike.
Even though he'll be out
before next year's carnival,
will he offer to do the work again?
Will he come to the carnival with us
to celebrate winter,
the outdoors,
and a free life?

29.

Maybe building an ice palace
in the dead of winter
and having a celebration
to break winter's chill
can stir up your interest in life again,
even though
once the weather gets warmer,
the palace gets smaller
and smaller
until one day
it's not there anymore at all,
and you wonder whether
it really existed,
or whether it was all
in your mind.

Every year since 1897 the small village of Saranac Lake, in northern New York State, has staged a winter carnival.

The carnival now lasts for ten days. Its crowning glory is the ice palace, a fantastical creation built on the banks of Lake Flower, just minutes from the town hall. It is made out of blocks carved from the frozen lake, up to 4,000 of them, each one weighing about 800 pounds.

Dr. Edward Livingston Trudeau, a doctor and sportsman who had contracted tuberculosis, came to the area in 1876 to live out what he thought would be his last months. He recovered, however, and in 1884 set up a sanitarium where other TB sufferers could benefit from rest in the clean mountain air. The first carnival was not only a festival to break the chill of winter but also a midwinter diversion to cheer the sick. The centerpiece of early carnivals was an ice tower, a far more modest creation than today's ice palace.

In the early 1980s a minimum-security correctional facility, Camp Gabriels, was established nearby. Around the country, inmates from minimum- and medium-security prisons were helping with community service, and the idea spread to Saranac Lake. Soon, crews of men—many in the upstate wilderness for the first time—were being let out every winter, under supervision, to work on the ice palace alongside people from the village. The partnership between the local community and the prison population means a great deal to both groups.

The work schedule depends on the weather. Winter temperatures in Saranac Village regularly drop below zero, with a record low of 35 below. Nowadays, though, with winters getting warmer amid signs of global warming, putting up the palace must sometimes be delayed until the ice becomes thick enough.

Tradition is a vital part of the carnival, and so is change. The planning committee designates a new theme each year—such as Cabin Fever or Boogie Down Broadway—and a new design for each palace, incorporating fables about a mythical mascot, Sara the Snowy Owl.

One part of the cycle remains the same every year. At the end of the carnival the ice palace, now deserted, gets smaller and smaller and finally melts away.